To:
Quincy & Reece

♡ Auntie Holly

For
Ari, Easton, Briella,
Mason,
and
Osh

**www.mascotbooks.com**

*A Normal Turtle*

**For more information, please contact:**
Mascot Books
560 Herndon Parkway #120
Herndon, VA 20170
info@mascotbooks.com

Library of Congress Control Number: 2017905036

CPSIA Code: PBANG0917A
ISBN-13: 978-1-68401-289-3

Printed in the United States

# <sup>a</sup>Normal turtle

written and illustrated by doug reynolds

This story is different from "normal," it's said,

A boy born as a fox, raised a turtle instead!

Of course, every person's unique in their way,

But a fox in a shell is our story today...

On his very first morning,
his very first dawn,
Our cute little kit woke
himself with a yawn.

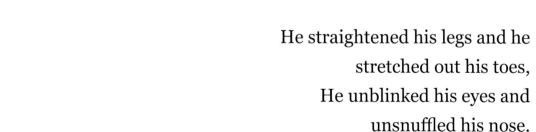

He straightened his legs and he
stretched out his toes,
He unblinked his eyes and
unsnuffled his nose.

He wiggled and waggled
and teetered, and then,
Without meaning to,
tumbled out of his den!

*boing*

He bounced off a **log**
and he rolled down a hill.
Getting knocked around silly,
as tumbling will.

*smack*

*thump thump*

At last his big fall
turned itself to a roll.
But before it would stop,
he **plopped** straight down a **hole!**

*plop*

Had he gone far?
He couldn't quite tell,
So he went back to sleep...

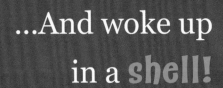

...And woke up
in a **shell!**

He couldn't recall,
had he traveled somewhere?
It's so hard when you're small
to tell this **here** from **there**.

As morning crept in and brought up the sun,
He found nothing strange when he saw everyone.

A nest full of turtles, as green as can be,
He didn't think odd as the first thing to see.

They woke and they ate
and they went for a swim,
And treated our fox
just like one of them.

He couldn't remember
a time before now,
So he thought himself turtle,
some way or some how...

It might not be easy for us to believe,
How one little fox had become so deceived,

But rather than picture a change in your day,
Imagine your life always being that way.

(If everyone else in your life had a shell,
You might not think twice if you wore one as well.)

But as the days passed, he started to find,
A strange little thought in the back of his mind.

It kept crying out, despite all his might,
That though nothing was wrong, somehow nothing seemed right...

He was still him — that he knew from the start,
But his outside seemed wrong, he could feel in his heart.

Something was off, something seemed out of place!
His reflection was not of a turtle-like face...

His shell was too loose, and his beak was too long,
He moved much too fast, and his tail looked all wrong.

He tried to adjust
and he tried to fit in,
Yet, felt so peculiar
time and again.

To be a good turtle,
one moved awful slow;
It took time to get going,
wherever they'd go.

And as he grew up, things just didn't change,
So to act like a turtle still felt rather strange.

His family loved fishing,
slept inside for fun;
Whereas he preferred pouncing,
and naps in the sun.

Still, he loved to run,
and to roll around too,

"But that is not what
normal turtles should do."

"Why not?" he would ask,
to which they'd reply,

"It's just not! That's just that,
and you shouldn't ask why."

But to act like a turtle, try as he might,
He could never perfect, and it never felt right.

It was silly to him, but he'd try and he'd try,
Just to feel broken, just to curl up and cry.

Our poor little friend had such a hard time,
Finding his reason and rhythm and rhyme.

His parents would say,
"We're so proud of you!
You're doing the things normal turtles *should* do."

But though he tried hard,
he couldn't escape,
He was a fox in his mind,
though a turtle in shape.

He said to his friend,
"I don't think this is me.
I think someone else
is who I'm s'posed to be..."

He sat and he thought and he mulled for a spell,
Until his friend said, "I always could tell,

You've never been happy
to hide who you are,
To pretend you're not you
hasn't helped out so far."

That was just it,
what he needed to hear —
And right then and there
he conquered his fear!

He stopped the whole act of moving so slow,
Instead now of hiding, he'd let it all show!
He jumped and he bounded and snuck through the grass,
He frolicked and wiggled and dug through the trash.

"Oh dear," his mother said, and his father did too,
"These are not normal things
for a turtle to do!"

It dawned on him now, he'd just had enough,
He couldn't keep doing that turtlish stuff!
He wasn't afraid anymore, he could tell,
So he took a deep breath...

...And came out of his shell!

# Everyone gasped!

But then some of them cheered...

It wasn't the tragedy he'd always feared!

So much better than that, so much better by far,
To hear:

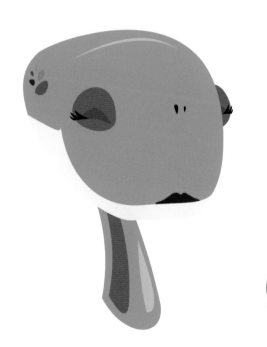

"We'll always love you, whoever you are."

When he heard those words,
he swelled up with **pride,**
Knowing he could be him,
no more having to hide.

And now he was faster than he'd ever been,
And in place of a frown, he was wearing a grin.

He started to yip, but it caught in his throat,
Even he had been stunned by his beautiful coat.

Right then every doubt, every fear he would fail,
Faded away as he flourished his tail.

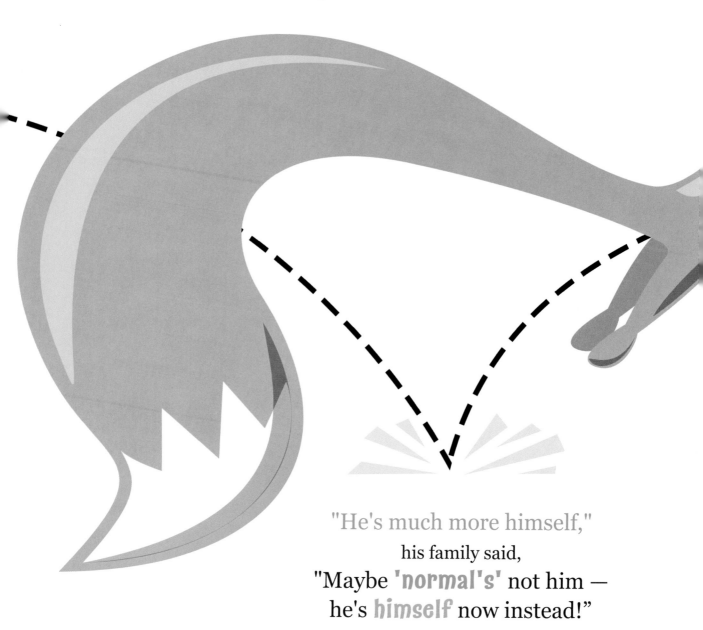

"He's much more himself,"
his family said,
"Maybe 'normal's' not him —
he's himself now instead!"

"For all of my life,
I've tried to pretend.
But being different than me,
didn't work in the end.

What's **'normal'** to some,
to another is not,
No use paying heed
to what everyone thought.

It's important, I think,
just to be who you are,
Being honest and true
is much better by far.

So don't be afraid,
things will turn out quite well,
When you're brave and you're ready...

Just COME OUT of your SHELL

So as he grew up, he remained, I am told,
A unique sort of *"turtle,"* until he was old.
So much of his life was filled up with laughter,
He happily lived forever and after.
He never again felt he needed to hide
The person he was on the in- or out-side.

Some *turtle*, some *fox*, to himself he was true,
Showing everyone else
what a turtle
can do.

A special thank you

**Craig Jessen**

For your input and guidance

**Craig Hudson**

For creating a safe space

and of course

**Jeri, Jessi, & Sam**

For your support, love,
& inspiration

This book is designed to help parents and educators teach lessons of love, acceptance, and empathy for those who are "different." But more importantly, to help all children feel safe being who they are.

For more information on how you can help at-risk LGBTQ kids, please visit TheTrevorProject.org.

If you need help urgently, please call the Trevor Project Lifeline at 1-866-488-7386

# About the Author

Author and illustrator Doug Reynolds' background
is in theatre, with a particular focus in performance,
Shakespeare, and playwriting.

Growing up gay in small-town America, Doug is intimately
aware of the specific challenges facing LGBTQ youth, even
in the 21st century. He has written this book as a gift to his
nieces and nephews in the hope that, with their parents'
support, it will help teach them tolerance of others and
acceptance of themselves, whoever they may be...

He lives in Portland, Oregon with his mongrel dog, Harper.

## Have a book idea?
### Contact us at:

info@mascotbooks.com | www.mascotbooks.com